Super Sweet Sleepy Slumber

Dedicated to Fred. The most awesome, sleepy cat in the whole wide world.

Super Sweet Sleepy Slumber
ISBN: 978-1-941775-09-7
April Chloe Terrazas
Copyright © 2014 Crazy Brainz, LLC

Visit us on the web! www.Crazy-Brainz.com

Cover design, illustrations and text by: April Chloe Terrazas

Sleepy Snake

<u>Position:</u> **Standing**

<u>Movement:</u> **Slowly bend and stretch your body like a sleepy snake.**

Breathe in and out <u>3 times</u> while moving.

Breathe in
3 seconds.
1....2....3....

Breathe out
4 seconds.
1....2....3....4....

Sleepy Cat

Position: **Standing**
Movement: **Reach for a star,
then reach down slowly
and touch your feet.**

**Breathe in 3 seconds reaching up,
breathe out 4 seconds reaching down.**

Repeat 3 times.

Sleepy Bear

<u>Position</u>: **Laying**

<u>Movement</u>: **On your back with your hands on your tummy.**

Take big, slow breaths.
Make your tummy rise as much as possible when you breathe in!

*Breathe in your nose
for 3 seconds.
1....2....3....*

*Breathe out your mouth
for 4 seconds.
1....2....3....4....*

Sleepy Mouse

Position: **Laying**

Movement: **Scoot up close to the wall with your legs going up the wall. The back of your legs should touch the wall just like the mouse's legs touch the cheese!**

Breathe in slowly 3 seconds.
_1....2....3...._
Breathe out slowly 4 seconds.
_1....2....3....4...._

Take 5 deep breaths with your legs up the wall.

Sleepy Giraffe

<u>Position:</u> **Laying**

<u>Movement</u>: **Lie on your back and hug your knees in to your chest. Bring your chin toward your knees. Squeeze your knees to your chest.**

Breathe in 3 seconds.
1....2....3....

While breathing out, stretch your legs out straight on the floor.
1....2....3....4....

Repeat 3 more times,
bring your legs to your chest,
then release back to the floor.

Sleepy Bunny

Position: **Laying**
Movement: **Lay your arms out to each side and drop both knees to one side.**

Breathe in 3 seconds.
Breathe out 4 seconds.

Keep your arms out to each side, bring your knees to the other side. Take a deep breath in and out.

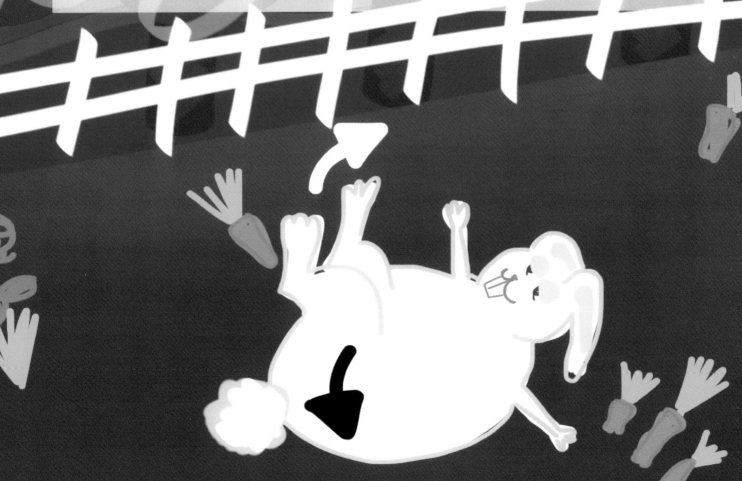

Sleepy Puppy

Position: **Laying**

Movement: **Hold your feet with your hands and rock side to side. Take 3 deep breaths.**

Breathe in 3 seconds.
1....2....3....

Breathe out 4 seconds.
1....2....3....4....

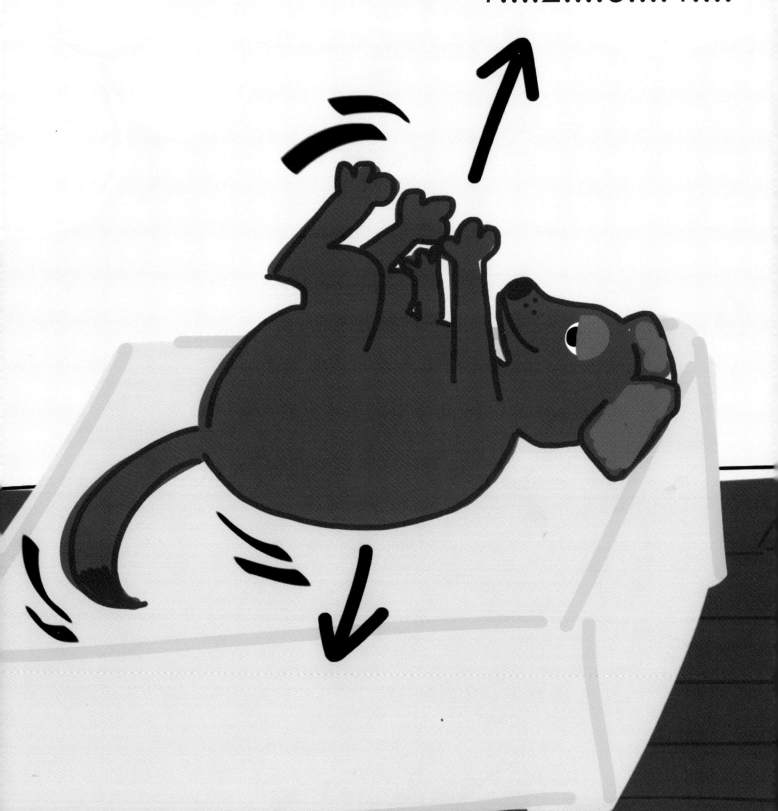

Sleepy Lion

Position: **Laying**

Movement: **Squeeze your body. Start with your fingers and your toes, then your arms and face... squeeze everything!**

Count to 5
1.....2.....3.....4.....5.....

Relax.
Take a deep breath in,
and a deep breath out.

Sleepy Octopus

Position: **Laying**

Movement: **Wiggle and shake your arms and legs slowly. Move your arms and legs in every direction.**

Breathe in 3 seconds. 1....2....3....
Breathe out 4 seconds. 1....2....3....4....

<u>Position</u>: **Standing or laying**

<u>Movement</u>:

Hug your mommy or daddy and relax while you breathe in 3 seconds..

1....2....3....

and breathe out 4 seconds..

1....2....3....4....

Sleepy Monkey

<u>Position</u>: **Laying**
<u>Movement</u>: **Relax and...**

Say goodnight to your toes,
Say goodnight to your feet,
Say goodnight to your tummy,
Say goodnight to your arms,
Say goodnight to your hands.

Breathe in 3 seconds..
1....2....3....

Breathe out 4 seconds..
1....2....3....4....

Sleepy Sheep

<u>*Position*</u>: **Laying**
<u>*Movement*</u>: **Relax**

Sleepy Sheep says:

I love to sleep
I sleep all night long

I love to sleep
I sleep happy and well

I love to sleep
I sleep all night long

I love to sleep
I sleep happy and well

GOODNIGHT

Create your own sleepy time move and draw a picture!